little Miss Naughty

by Roger Hargreaves

Are you ever naughty?

Sometimes, I bet!

Well, Little Miss Naughty was naughty all the time.

She awoke one Sunday morning and looked out of the window.

"Looks like a nice day," she thought to herself.

And then she grinned.

"Looks like a nice day for being naughty," she said.

And rubbed her hands!

That Sunday Mr Uppity was out for his morning stroll.

Little Miss Naughty knocked his hat off his head.

And jumped on it!

"My hat!" cried Mr Uppity.

That afternoon Mr Clever was sitting in his garden reading a book.

And do you know what that Little Miss Naughty did?

She broke his glasses!

"My glasses!" cried Mr Clever.

That evening Mr Bump was just standing there.

Minding his own business.

And guess what Little Miss Naughty did?

She ran off with his bandages!

And bandaged up Mr Small!

"Mmmmmmmmmmffffff!" he cried.

It's difficult to say anything when you're bandaged up like that!

Mr Uppity and Mr Clever and Mr Bump and Mr Small were very very very very cross.

Very very very very cross indeed!

"Oh what a wonderful Sunday," giggled Little Miss Naughty as she walked along.

"And it isn't even bedtime yet!"

First thing on Monday morning the Mr Men had a meeting.

"Something has to be done," announced Mr Uppity, who had managed to straighten out his hat.

They all looked at Mr Clever, who was wearing his spare pair of glasses.

"You're the cleverest," they said. "What's to be done about Little Miss Naughty?"

Mr Clever thought.

He cleared his throat.

And spoke.

"I've no idea," he said.

"I have," piped up Mr Small.

"I know what that naughty little lady needs," he went on.

"And I know who can do it," he added.

"What?" asked Mr Uppity.

"Who?" asked Mr Clever.

"Aha!" chuckled Mr Small, and went off to see a friend of his.

Somebody who could do impossible things.

Somebody who could do impossible things like making himself invisible.

I wonder who that could be?

That Monday Mr Nosey was asleep under a tree.

Little Miss Naughty crept towards him with a pot of paint in one hand, a paintbrush in the other, and a rather large grin on her face.

She was going to paint the end of his nose!

Red!

But.

Just as she was about to do the dreadful deed, something happened.

TWEAK!

Somebody tweaked her nose!

Somebody she couldn't see tweaked her nose!

Somebody invisible!

I wonder who?

"Ouch!" cried Little Miss Naughty.

And, dropping the paint and paintbrush, she ran away as fast as her little legs would carry her.

On Tuesday Mr Busy was rushing along.

As usual!

Little Miss Naughty, standing by the side of the road, stuck out her foot.

She was going to trip him up!

Head over heels!

And heels over head!

But.

Just before she did, something happened.

TWEAK!

The invisible nose tweaker had struck again!

And it hurt!

"Ouch!" cried Little Miss Naughty.

And ran away even faster than her little legs would carry her.

On Wednesday Mr Happy was at home.

Watching television!

Outside, Little Miss Naughty picked up a stone.

She was going to break his window!

Naughty girl!

But.

As she brought her arm back to throw, guess what?

That's right!

TWEAK!

"Ouch!" cried Little Miss Naughty as she ran off holding her nose.

And so it went on.

All day Thursday.

TWEAK!

All day Friday.

TWEAK! TWEAK!

All day Saturday.

TWEAK! TWEAK! TWEAK!

By which time Little Miss Naughty's nose was bright red.

But.

By Sunday she was cured.

No naughtiness at all!

Thanks to the invisible nose tweaker.

On Sunday evening Mr Small went round to see him.

"Hello Mr Impossible," he smiled.

"Thank you for helping to cure Little Miss Naughty."

"My pleasure," laughed Mr Impossible.

"But it did take all week."

Mr Small grinned.

"Don't you mean," he said, "all tweak?"

Fantastic offers for Little Miss fans!

Collect all your Mr. Men or Little Miss books in these superb durable collectors' cases!

Only £5.99 inc. postage and packing, these wipe-clean, hard-wearing cases will give all your Mr. Men or Little Miss books a beautiful new home!

Keep track of your collection with this giant-sized double-sided Mr. Men and Little Miss Collectors' poster.

Collect 6 tokens and we will send you a brilliant giant-sized double-sided collectors' poster! Simply tape a £1 coin to cover postage and packaging in the space provided and fill out the form overleaf.

STICK £1 COIN HERE (for poster only)

Only need a few Little Miss or Mr. Men to complete your set? You can order any of the titles on the back of the books from our Mr. Men order line on 0870 787 1724. Orders should be delivered between 5 and 7 working days.

──────── **TO BE COMPLETED BY AN ADULT** ────────

To apply for any of these great offers, ask an adult to complete the details below and send this whole page with the appropriate payment and tokens, to: MR. MEN CLASSIC OFFER, PO BOX 715, HORSHAM RH12 5WG

☐ Please send me a giant-sized double-sided collectors' poster.
AND ☐ I enclose 6 tokens and have taped a £1 coin to the other side of this page.

☐ Please send me ☐ Mr. Men Library case(s) and/or ☐ Little Miss library case(s) at £5.99 each inc P&P

☐ I enclose a cheque/postal order payable to Egmont UK Limited for £......................

OR ☐ Please debit my MasterCard / Visa / Maestro / Delta account (delete as appropriate) for £......................

Card no. ☐☐☐☐☐☐☐☐☐☐☐☐☐☐☐☐☐☐☐ Security code ☐☐☐

Issue no. (if available) ☐ Start Date ☐☐/☐☐/☐☐ Expiry Date ☐☐/☐☐/☐☐

Fan's name: .... Date of birth: ....

Address: ....

....

.... Postcode: ....

Name of parent / guardian: ....

Email for parent / guardian: ....

Signature of parent / guardian: ....

Please allow 28 days for delivery. Offer is only available while stocks last. We reserve the right to change the terms of this offer at any time and we offer a 14 day money back guarantee. This does not affect your statutory rights. Offers apply to UK only.

☐ We may occasionally wish to send you information about other Egmont children's books.
If you would rather we didn't, please tick this box.

Ref: LIM 001

cut along the dotted line and return this whole page